Too Many Ponies

Do you love ponies? Be a Pony Pal!

PONY PALS

Too Many Ponies

Jeanne Betancourt

illustrated by Paul Bachem

A
LITTLE APPLE
PAPERBACK

SCHOLASTIC INC.
New York Toronto London Auckland Sydney

ISBN 0-590-25245-3

Text copyright © 1995 by Jeanne Betancourt.
Illustrations copyright © 1995 by Scholastic Inc.
All rights reserved. Published by Scholastic Inc.
APPLE PAPERBACKS® is a registered trademark of Scholastic Inc.

31 30 29 28 27   5 6 7 8 9/0

Printed in the U.S.A.   40

First Scholastic printing, September 1995

For the original Pony Pal, Jean Feiwel

The author thanks Maria Genovesi, Elvia Gignoux, and Maria Nation for applying their knowledge of horses to this story.

Thanks also to Helen Perelman for her smart and sensitive editing.

Contents

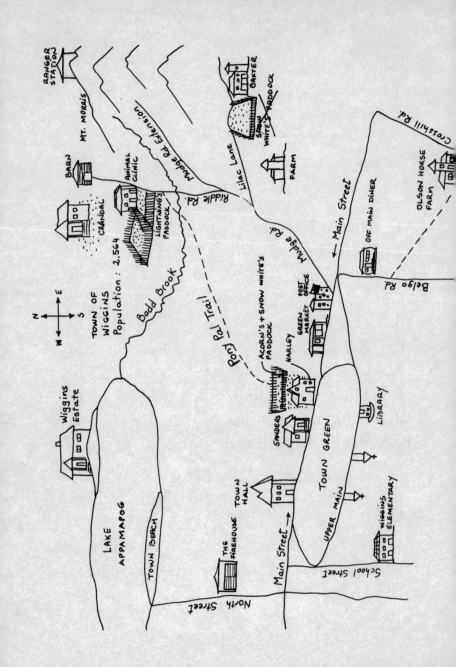

Pam's New Job

Lightning was grazing under the big maple tree. "Hey, girl," Pam Crandal called. The pony looked up and trotted over to meet her. Lightning's chestnut coat was the same reddish-brown color as the autumn leaves on the maple tree.

The pony gently nudged Pam's shoulder and whinnied a hello. Pam rubbed Lightning's muzzle. "Good pony," she said.

Pam took an apple from her pocket and gave it to Lightning. While the pony ate the treat, Pam watched the two ponies in

the next paddock. Pam's mother was a riding instructor so there were always horses at the Crandals'. This year Mrs. Crandal had many young students and needed more ponies. Pam had gone with her mother to help pick out two ponies at Mr. Olson's horse farm. Pam was happy to see the ponies grazing in the paddock.

Lightning nudged at Pam's bulging jacket pocket. Pam rubbed the pretty white marking on her pony's forehead. "No more for you," she said. "Too many apples can make you sick."

Pam left Lightning and slipped through the fence rails into the next paddock. The two new ponies, Splash and Daisy, didn't come to greet her. And Pam didn't approach them. Instead she held out an apple in each hand and waited.

Splash trotted over to Pam, grabbed his apple, and returned to the other side of the field. Pam loved how the Appaloosa pony's markings on his back looked like splatters of paint.

Daisy, meanwhile, took cautious steps in Pam's direction. "Here, Daisy," Pam said to the little palomino Shetland. "This one's for you." Daisy came closer and lifted the apple daintily out of Pam's hand.

Pam's mother was watching from the fence. "I'm glad Splash and Daisy are getting to know you," she told Pam.

"It's fun to have them here," said Pam.

"I need you to work them with me," her mother said. "I'm too tall to ride them."

Pam remembered how she rode each of the ponies around Mr. Olson's riding ring while her mother watched. Pam and her mother agreed that both ponies were well-trained. But Pam knew that the ponies would need more schooling.

"We'll have to work them a lot before my young students ride them," Pam's mother explained. "I have many beginning riders this year."

Pam rubbed Daisy's golden-colored muzzle. "I'll help you, Mom," she said.

"I'll pay you," her mother said.

"Maybe I'll finally save enough money to buy a new saddle," said Pam.

Pam had been using a second-hand saddle for five years. The old saddle was looking worn-out and Pam wanted a new one. The saddle she'd seen at Mr. Olson's was perfect. It was shiny dark-brown leather, didn't have any worn spots, and was the perfect size for her and Lightning.

Mrs. Crandal interrupted Pam's saddle-thoughts. "We should start working Splash and Daisy this morning," she said. "Okay?"

"Sure," Pam said. "I was going trail riding with Anna and Lulu. But I'll tell them I can't go." Pam knew when her friends heard she had a job training ponies, they'd understand.

"Bring Splash to the barn in ten minutes then," Pam's mother said.

Pam sat on the fence between the two paddocks and did some math. How much had she already saved toward a saddle? How much more did she need for the beautiful one she'd seen at Mr. Olson's?

Pam stopped doing her math problem when she heard Lightning's happy neigh. She looked up and saw Anna and Lulu coming off the trail on their ponies, Acorn and Snow White.

Anna and Lulu dismounted their ponies and led them through the paddock gate. By then Lightning had reached them and the three ponies were nickering and nipping at one another happily.

Pam met her friends and their ponies halfway across the field.

"It's a perfect day for riding," Lulu told Pam.

"I can't wait to get on those Mudge Road trails," Anna said.

"Come see the new ponies first," said Pam.

When the three girls and their ponies reached the fence, Anna exclaimed, "They're so *cute!*"

"Daisy's a true palomino color," said Lulu.

"She's sweet, too," Pam told her friends. "They're both great ponies."

"How are they getting along with Lightning?" asked Lulu.

"We haven't put them together yet," Pam said. "But they've been visiting over the fence."

"I think Lightning would rather be with Snow White and Acorn," said Anna.

Pam agreed with Anna. Like the Pony Pals, their three ponies were best friends. Pam rubbed Lightning's long, sleek neck. "You'll be with Acorn and Snow White tonight," she told her pony. "We're having a barn sleepover."

"They'll be together all day, too," Lulu reminded Pam, "while we're trail riding. So let's go. Saddle up."

"I'm going to help my mother work with the new ponies," Pam said. "And guess what? She's going to pay me. I'll have enough money for a new saddle a lot sooner than I thought. And Mr. Olson's got one for sale that's perfect for me. It's used, but it looks like new."

The Pony Pals hit high fives all around and shouted, "All right!"

"My job starts today," Pam said. "So I can't go riding with you."

"But we planned it," Anna said. "We're going on the Mudge Road trails."

"My dad told me about an old town that used to be over there," Lulu said. "We're going to look for the places the houses used to be."

At that moment, Pam's mother shouted to her from the barn. "Pam, catch Splash and bring him in. We'll work him first."

"Okay," Pam called back.

"We could wait for you," Lulu said.

"I've got two ponies to work," Pam said. "It'll be a long time."

"You mean you can't trail ride at all today?" Anna said.

Pam nodded.

"So I guess we'll go without you," Lulu said unhappily.

"But you'll be back here later," Pam reminded her friends, "for supper and our barn sleepover. We'll have fun."

"Sure," Anna said.

"See you later," said Lulu.

Lulu and Anna led their ponies out onto Riddle Road, and Pam went to fetch the new pony. She was thinking about how she would catch Splash, when she heard Lightning snort. She looked across the paddock. Lightning was pounding up and down the fence line bordering Riddle Road. The pony snorted again. What was wrong with Lightning?

Left Behind

Pam ran across the paddock. "Lightning. Lightning, it's okay," she called to the pony.

The unhappy pony ignored Pam and kept rushing up and down the fence line. Pam could see that Lightning wanted to go with Acorn and Snow White.

Even the family dog, Woolie, knew Lightning was upset. Woolie wasn't running alongside Lightning the way he usually did. Instead, he sat next to Pam, whimpering. Pam patted the dog's head and told him that everything would be all right.

When Anna and Lulu and their ponies were out of sight, Lightning finally stopped carrying on and slowly walked over to Pam.

Pam lay her head against her pony's hot side. She heard and felt Lightning's heartbeat racing. "I'm sorry," she said.

Lightning looked toward Riddle Road and neighed.

"I know," Pam said. "They're my best friends, too. We'll all be together tonight."

As Pam comforted her pony, she thought about her Pony Pals, Anna Harley and Lulu Sanders.

Pam and Anna met in kindergarten. On that first day of school, Anna had finger-painted a big red and yellow pony. Pam told Anna she was the best artist in the class. They talked about ponies the whole day. And became best friends.

Pam knew how lucky she was that her parents loved ponies as much as she did. Her mother taught horseback riding and her father was a veterinarian. And Pam had a pony for as long as she could remember. But Anna didn't have a pony until she was ten. Which was around the time that Pam and Anna met Lulu Sanders and Snow White.

Lulu came to Wiggins to live with her grandmother while her father studied animals in far-off places. But now Mr. Sanders was in Wiggins writing an article about black bears. Pam was glad Lulu and her father were together again. Lulu's mother died when she was little, and Lulu and her dad were especially close.

Anna and Lulu kept their ponies in a paddock behind Anna's house. A mile-and-a-half woodland trail — Pony Pal Trail — connected that paddock to Lightning's paddock at the Crandals'. So it was easy for the Pony Pals to visit one another on horseback.

Pam saw her mother waving to her from the barn doorway. "Haven't you caught Splash yet?" she yelled.

"Coming," Pam shouted back.

Pam looked into Lightning's eyes. Her pony had calmed down and was breathing normally again. "I'm sorry you can't be with your friends," she told Lightning. "But I've got a job. Pretty soon we'll have enough money for a new saddle for us. You'll love that."

Splash was standing at the fence between the paddocks waiting for Lightning. Pam thought she'd have trouble catching Splash. But with Lightning beside her it would be easy.

While the two ponies sniffed each other, Pam slipped through the fence and clipped a lead rope on Splash's halter. She reached over and she patted Lightning's cheek. "Thanks for helping," she said. Then she led Splash to the barn.

Pam knew she had to forget about Lightning now. If she was going to school Splash, she had to give him all of her attention. Pam talked gently to Splash and gave him friendly pats while she groomed and saddled him.

When Pam led the new pony outside, she saw her mother waiting for her in the center of the outdoor ring. Pam swung herself up on Splash's back.

"Start with a walk," Mrs. Crandal directed.

Everything went fine during the walk. But when Pam was doing a posting trot, she felt that her stirrups weren't right. She moved Splash back down to a walk, then brought him to a halt. "I need to lengthen my stirrups," she told her mother.

Mrs. Crandal and Pam were adjusting Pam's stirrups when the five-year-old Crandal twins, Jack and Jill, came running over to them.

"Can I ride Splash?" Jack asked.

"Me, too?" Jill said.

"I have to work him before any kids ride him," Pam told them.

"What have you been doing?" Mrs. Crandal asked the twins.

"Chasing mice," Jill said.

"Isn't that a job for the barn cats?" their mother asked.

"They're sleeping," Jack said.

"Where did you see mice?" Pam wanted to know.

"In the feed room," said Jill.

"I noticed some droppings in there this morning," Pam told her mother. "I think Jezebel and No Tail are bored with catching mice."

"I think they've turned into lazy cats," Mrs. Crandal said. "Maybe after all these years they've retired." She sighed. "But we'll worry about that later. Right now, let's get back to work with Splash."

The twins left the ring and Pam worked Splash in a walk and trot. When she directed the pony to go back to a walk, Splash continued to trot. Pam was firm with the pony and he finally slowed down.

"Good work, Pam," her mother said. "You're great at this."

"Thanks," Pam said.

Pam noticed Lightning standing at the

fence staring at her. Is Lightning jealous that I'm riding Splash? she wondered.

Just then a truck going along Riddle Road backfired. Splash was spooked by the sudden noise and stumbled. Pam lost her balance for a split second. But she caught herself and regained balance as she reined in the frightened pony.

"Pam," her mother scolded, "you need to stay focused."

"Sorry," Pam said.

I have to stop worrying about Lightning, Pam thought. I've got to pay attention to my job.

Fat Cat

After lunch, Pam went back out to the paddocks to get Daisy for *her* lesson. When Pam called out "Daisy," the pony looked in Pam's direction and took a step backward. She's very shy, Pam thought. I hope she's not hard to catch. Pam put her hand behind her back so Daisy wouldn't see she was carrying a lead rope.

Meanwhile, Lightning was getting as close to Pam as possible. She stuck her muzzle through the fence rails and nudged at the lead rope and nickered. To Pam, Lightning seemed to be saying, "Don't take that other pony. Take me."

"Sorry, Lightning," she said, "I *have* to ride Daisy. It's my job."

Pam talked quietly to Daisy and the pony stayed still for her. Pam clipped the lead rope to Daisy's halter and led her toward the barn. Lightning followed them to the gate.

After Daisy's lesson, Pam sat on the fence and pushed her fingers through Lightning's red mane. Pam knew that her new job was confusing Lightning. "And you miss Acorn and Snow White," Pam said. "Now that I'm finished working for today, I miss them, too."

Pam kept looking over to Riddle Road. Soon two ponies and their riders came into view.

"They're back," she told Lightning excitedly. "Let's go meet them."

Pam tied the lead rope to Lightning's halter and heaved herself on her bare back. Lightning nickered happily, stretched out her sleek body, and cantered toward the paddock gate.

As Pam slid off Lightning's back she saw that a big gray cat was walking beside Acorn and Anna.

"Where'd that cat come from?" Pam asked.

"We found him on Mudge Road," Lulu said.

"It's the biggest cat I've ever seen," Pam said.

"He followed us," said Anna. "But something's wrong with his leg. He limps. We thought your dad should look at him."

Pam picked up the cat and stroked its soft gray coat. "He's so furry," she said.

"And fat," Lulu added.

While Anna and Lulu unsaddled their ponies, Pam put the cat in the barn office. Then she went to get her dad from the animal clinic.

By the time Pam and Dr. Crandal came into the barn, Anna, Lulu, Jack, Jill, Mrs. Crandal, and Woolie were crowded in the

office. The gray cat, sitting on Mrs. Crandal's desk chair, was the center of everyone's attention.

"Well," Dr. Crandal said, "what have we here?"

"A cat," said Jill. "Anna and Lulu found him. He doesn't have a tag."

"His name is Fat Cat," Jack announced. "I named him."

"Me, too!" Jill added.

"Well, Mr. Fat Cat," Dr. Crandal said, "let's take a look at you." Dr. Crandal picked up the cat and checked him over. "She's purring like a motorboat," he said with a smile.

" 'She'?" Pam said with surprise. "He's a she?"

"Fat Cat is not only a female cat," Dr. Crandal told them, "she's a pregnant cat."

"Pregnant means she's going to have kittens," Pam told Jill.

"I *know* that," Jill said.

"What about her leg?" Anna asked.

"Her leg is a little swollen," Dr. Crandal

said. "She must have sprained it. But it's nothing to worry about. It's the sort of injury that fixes itself."

"What are we going to do with another cat?" Mrs. Crandal wondered out loud. "And then kittens!"

Fat Cat suddenly jumped out of Dr. Crandal's arms and raced around the room.

"Look!" Anna squealed. "She's chasing a mouse."

"I see it!" Lulu shouted. "It's going under the door."

Mrs. Crandal quickly opened the door. The cat streaked out of the office to continue the chase down the barn aisle. Woolie cheered Fat Cat on with an enthusiastic bark.

Everyone laughed.

"Fat Cat," Mrs. Crandal said, "you've got yourself a job."

"And a new home," Pam added.

After a spaghetti dinner with the Crandals, the three friends went out to the barn.

They got the tack room ready for their sleepover by laying out their sleeping bags side by side. Then they went out and sat on the fence.

The paddocks were lit by the white light of a full moon. The Pony Pals watched Acorn and Lightning trot toward the big maple tree. Snow White followed at a slower pace. When the faster ponies reached the tree, they turned around and went back to get Snow White.

"They're great friends," Anna remarked. "Just like us."

Meanwhile Daisy and Splash grazed at the far side of their own paddock. Pam told Anna and Lulu about her training sessions with Splash and Daisy. "I'm getting to know them," she said. "Splash has lots of energy. But I think he's used to getting away with stuff."

"What about the Shetland?" Anna asked. "Is Daisy a lot like Acorn?"

"She's sweet like Acorn," said Pam, "so

I think she'll be great with little kids. But she's lazy and slow. My job is to get her to work harder."

Pam wanted to keep talking about her job and the saddle she was going to buy with the money she made. But Lulu changed the subject. "We found the neatest place today," she said.

"Wait until you see it, Pam," Anna said. "It's ancient. We went where Lulu's dad said there once was a farm. And we found where a house used to be."

"There's a big hole in the ground with rock walls," Lulu said. "It used to be a cellar."

"We explored in there for the longest time," Anna added. "I want to go back and dig in the ground. I bet we'll find pieces of stuff they used in that house."

"We'll go tomorrow," Lulu told Pam, "and show you."

"I can't," Pam said. "I'm working with the new ponies."

"*Again!*" Anna wailed. "That's awful."

"That means you're not riding with us at all this weekend," Lulu complained.

"I can't help it," Pam said.

The three girls were silent. After a while they went to the barn and got ready for bed. Pam was the first to get into her sleeping bag. Suddenly she jumped up screaming. "Some*thing* — is — in — there," she stuttered.

The Pony Pals ran to the door. They stared at the sleeping bag. It moved.

"What is it?" Anna whispered.

"Maybe it's a racoon," Lulu said.

They saw a bit of fur at the opening of the sleeping bag. Then more fur. A big gray cat crawled all the way out.

"Fat Cat!" the girls squealed.

Fat Cat looked around as if to ask, "What's all the fuss about?"

The Pony Pals ran back into the room and collapsed in a giggling heap on top of Pam's sleeping bag. Fat Cat rubbed against them, swished her furry tail, and purred.

Pam was still giggling when she picked up the cat and put her in the feed room. "You have work to do tonight, Fat Cat," she said. "Go scare mice instead of people." She closed the door to the tack room so Fat Cat wouldn't come back to the barn sleepover party.

The girls got settled in their sleeping bags. "I wish you could come with us tomorrow, Pam," Lulu said.

"I thought being Pony Pals meant we rode together," said Anna.

Pam didn't say anything. She was thinking about how much she liked her job training Splash and Daisy.

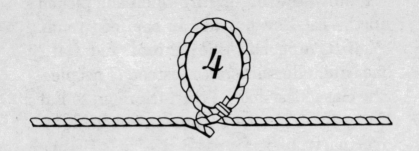

Splash's Trail Ride

Every day after school for a week, Pam worked the new ponies in the ring. She was very tired. But when Pam heard Woolie's bark early Saturday morning, she jumped right out of bed anyway. She wanted to get her barn chores done early today. This morning and all weekend she was going riding with her friends.

Pam walked out to the paddock where Lightning and the two new ponies had spent the night. All three ponies came running toward her. Lightning reached her first. While Pam gave her pony a special good-morning hug, Splash came over and tried to nudge his way between Lightning and Pam. Pam gave him a friendly pat on the muzzle. Then she turned her attention to Daisy who waited shyly behind the other two ponies.

Pam went to the feed room to get oats. The enormous gray cat was sitting on the feed box, alert to every little movement and sound. There isn't a mouse in Wiggins who would dare to enter this room, Pam thought.

Pam scratched the cat behind the ears. "Good job, Fat Cat," she said. Fat Cat purred her thanks, then jumped off the feed box so Pam could open it.

When Pam had finished feeding the ponies, she checked the chart she'd made for schooling Splash. She needed to make sure that Splash would be ready for her mother's students.

TRAINING CHART
SPLASH

NW = needs work
G = good
VG = very good

	Sa	Su	M	T	W	Th	F
stands still for mount	G	G	G	VG	VG	VG	VG
halt	NW	G	VG	VG	NW	G	VG
walk	G	G	G	G	G	G	G
trot	G	G	VG	VG	VG	VG	VG
canter	VG	VG	VG	VG	VG	VG	VG
jumps	—	—	—	G	G	VG	VG
transitions	NW	NW	NW	NW	NW	G	G
on trail alone	—	—	—	—	—	—	VG
on trail in group	—	—	—	—	—	—	—

comments: spooked when truck back fired   doesn't like to slow down   needs to ride on trail with other ponies

Pam saw that she needed to take Splash trail riding in a group. If I take Splash out today with my friends, she thought, I'd be working and playing at the same time. Her mother agreed with the plan.

A few minutes later, Pam led Lightning to the barn. Instead of tacking her up, she put her in a stall in the back. "I know you like it better outside," she said. "But you'll only be here for a little while."

Pam returned to the paddock, caught Splash, and saddled him up. She asked her mother to let Lightning out after she left. "Lightning would be so upset that I'm trail riding on Splash instead of her," she explained.

"I'll put her back out in the paddock with Daisy as soon as you're out of sight," her mother promised. "And remember," she added, "stick to Pony Pal Trail until you're sure Splash is okay riding in a group."

As Pam rode Splash along the trail, she noticed how much the pony had improved in the one week she'd been working with him. Now when she asked him to slow down he responded quickly. And when a squirrel streaked across the trail he didn't spook.

Pam couldn't believe she could be having so much fun and getting paid for it! "You're a terrific little pony," she told Splash. "And you're a good ride."

Pam was the first to reach the Pony Pal meeting place at the three white birch trees. She hadn't told Anna and Lulu that she'd be riding Splash instead of Lightning. But she knew they'd understand. Working Splash on the trail was part of her job.

When Snow White and Acorn appeared around the bend of the trail, Anna said, "Where's Lightning?"

"Is she sick?" asked Lulu.

"Lightning's fine," Pam said. "I have to work Splash on the trail with other ponies."

Splash whinnied and pulled up against the bit. Pam pulled him in sharply. "He doesn't usually do that," she said. "We better stick to Pony Pal Trail for awhile."

"Then let's go back to that old town," Anna said.

Lulu patted the short shovel she'd tied to the back of her saddle. "We'll do a dig," she said, "like archaeologists."

"I have to stick around here with Splash," Pam said. "We haven't checked him on a road with cars yet. We can bring him over there another time."

"Aren't you ever going to ride Lightning again?" Anna asked.

"Of course," Pam said. "Lightning's my pony. But right now I *have* to ride Splash."

Acorn pawed at the ground restlessly. Snow White neighed. They missed Lightning, too.

"We'd better get these ponies moving," said Lulu.

"Lulu, it's your turn to take the lead," Pam said.

Lulu directed Snow White to move forward.

Anna followed on Acorn.

Pam and Splash took up the rear.

Lulu started them out at a walk, but Splash immediately wanted to trot. When Pam tried to hold him in the walk, he did a jig in place. It was as difficult to hold him back as on the first day she worked him.

"Come on, Splash," Pam scolded, "behave yourself."

Splash's ears went back, and he scooted. In a split second he'd covered the space between himself and Acorn. Acorn whinnied his disapproval and tried to turn on Splash. Anna struggled to keep Acorn in check. Meanwhile, Splash was tossing his head and snorting.

"Don't let him crowd," Anna shouted to Pam as she finally got Acorn to move forward again. "Keep the space between them."

"Sorry," Pam said. "Maybe if you guys go a little faster it'll work better."

Lulu moved Snow White through a trot into a canter. Acorn followed at the same speed. But Splash still strained to go faster than the ponies ahead of him.

"*Whoa!*" Pam shouted at the pony. She pulled hard on the reins until Splash finally stopped. "That's enough," she scolded.

Pam was panting hard from the effort of controlling Splash and she felt the sweat under the rim of her hat. Splash was breathing hard and sweating, too.

All three girls dismounted. Lulu walked over to Pam while Anna held Acorn and Snow White a safe distance away from Splash.

"This is a bad idea," Lulu told Pam. "It's dangerous for us to ride with Splash."

"He was *perfect* yesterday," Pam said.

"Why don't you bring him back and get Lightning," Lulu suggested. "Then the day won't be ruined. We'll wait for you."

"If I put Splash out in the paddock for the rest of the day he'll think it's a reward for his bad behavior," Pam explained. "Then he'll be even worse the next time he goes on the trail with other horses."

"Promise you won't bring Splash the next time we ride," Anna said.

"I promise," Pam told her.

"Good!" Lulu said. "Then maybe things will go back to normal."

Pam hoped that she could keep her promise to her friends and her job.

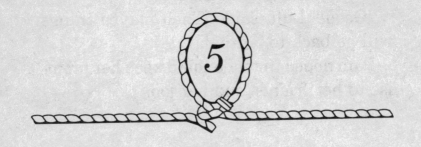

The Fight

Sunday morning Mrs. Crandal handed Pam her first week's salary. After breakfast Pam ran up to her room and took her barn bank down from the top bookshelf. She opened the roof, took out the money she'd already saved, and counted it. Great, she thought, if I work every day pretty soon I'll have enough for that new saddle.

Pam walked into the kitchen to find her mother. "I want to work today, too," Pam told her.

"I thought we'd all take today off," Mrs. Crandal said.

"But I haven't ridden Daisy on the trail yet," Pam said.

"What about Lightning?" Mrs. Crandal asked. "I thought you were taking her out today."

"I can ride her when I get back," Pam said.

After Pam put Lightning in a stall in the back of the barn, she went to the front to groom and saddle up Daisy.

Daisy nickered cheerfully when Pam rode her onto Pony Pal Trail. The palomino pony seemed to be saying, "I like it here. This is a very pretty place." She liked the trail so much that she wanted to stop to admire every falling leaf and chirping bird. Pam let the pony take her time so she'd get used to the trail. She figured Daisy would happily move into the trot and canter when she was behind fast-moving Acorn and Snow White.

Pam saw Anna and Lulu waiting for her at their birch tree meeting place. She waved and they waved back. But Anna was frowning and Lulu was twisting her mouth the way she did when she was angry.

"Why didn't you tell us you were riding Daisy today?" Anna asked as Pam rode up to her.

"I didn't decide until this morning," Pam said.

"Don't let Daisy get too close to Snow White," Lulu ordered.

"Daisy won't act like Splash did yesterday," Pam said. "Stop worrying."

Acorn took a step forward and nickered a friendly hello to Daisy.

"See," said Pam. "They like Daisy. She'll be great with them on the trail. And she'll never try to rush ahead like Splash did."

"Lightning must hate that you keep leaving her behind," said Anna.

"She doesn't know," Pam said. "I put her in the barn, then my mom lets her out when I'm gone."

"I bet Lightning still knows," Lulu said. "She's smart. You can't fool her."

Pam didn't want to feel guilty about Lightning. She was riding Daisy today and it was Daisy she had to think about. "Let's just ride, okay?" she said.

The three girls moved their ponies onto the trail. Anna was in the lead. Lulu came next. Pam and Daisy brought up the rear.

When the ponies walked, everything was fine. "I told you she'd be okay," Pam shouted ahead to her friends.

Anna moved Acorn into a lively trot. Snow White followed. But Daisy had a slower trot and soon she was lagging behind. When the other ponies cantered, Daisy fell even farther behind.

I have to let Daisy know what I want and be firm, Pam reminded herself. She gave all her attention to the lazy pony, but it didn't make much difference.

By the time Pam caught up with her Pony Pals they had reached Badd Brook. Anna and Lulu were sitting on a big rock and having a snack while their ponies were drinking from the brook.

"Daisy is such a slowpoke," Pam said as she led the pony to the stream.

"She sure is different from Splash," said Lulu.

"And Lightning," Anna added. "I miss Lightning."

"What should we do next?" Lulu asked.

"I wanted to go back to that old house," Anna said. "But I guess we can't with Daisy."

"There's plenty to do around here," Pam said. "We always have fun on the Wiggins Estate trails."

"I just hate it when we plan something and then can't do it," complained Lulu.

No one said anything for awhile.

Anna finished her snack and brushed the crumbs off her jacket. "It's like you're not even a Pony Pal anymore," she mumbled.

"Anna, that's a dumb thing to say," said Pam. "Why'd you say that?"

"Because you're forgetting all about

Lightning," Anna said. "And the Pony Pals."

"And you keep doing things without telling us," said Lulu. "Like bringing these other ponies on our rides."

"And then we can't do what we said we'd do. Like going to that old farm," Anna said.

"I have a job," Pam said in an angry voice. "I can't *play* all the time like you."

"Pam, you're working too hard," Lulu said. "You never just have fun anymore."

Pam jumped up. "You guys are jealous that I have a job and you don't," she said.

"That's ridiculous," said Lulu. "I am not jealous."

"Me either," Anna said. "Who'd want to turn into a grump like you?"

"I'm not a grump," shouted Pam. "You guys are the grumps. You're the ones who are complaining all the time. You're the ones who are being selfish and mean!"

Anna folded her arms and turned her back to Pam. Lulu picked up some pebbles and started thowing them, one by one, into the water.

Pam wanted to get away from Anna and Lulu as fast as she could. She ran over to Daisy and put on the bridle. Anna and Lulu still ignored her. Pam mounted the pony. "Now you can go play in that stupid old house," she told them.

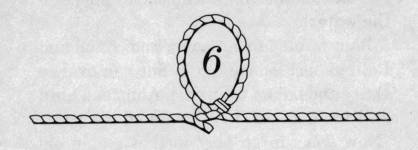

Keep Away

Pam rode through the woods toward Pony Pal Trail. She wanted to get far away from her *former* friends. But Daisy was the slowest pony she ever rode.

Lightning would be thrilled to move into a gallop. It was much more fun to ride her own pony. On Lightning she would feel as if she were *flying* over the open stretch of trail.

When Pam reached the paddock gate, she saw that her pony was in the run-in shed at the other end of the field. She took the long way to the barn so Lightning wouldn't see her on another pony.

Pam took off Daisy's tack and cooled her down. She couldn't wait to finish with this pony so she could take Lightning for a ride on Pony Pal Trail.

But thinking about the trail reminded her of the good times she had riding with Anna and Lulu.

Pam thought about their ponies' happy whinnies and the sound of hooves pounding along the trail. She remembered their Pony Pal adventures and some of the difficult problems they'd solved together. Mostly she remembered how special and wonderful it felt to be a Pony Pal.

Why did Anna and Lulu have to go ruin the Pony Pals by being jealous? Pam was so angry at Anna and Lulu that she wanted to scream.

After putting Daisy in the side paddock with Splash, Pam went to get Lightning. She and Lightning would go for a ride alone. She didn't need Pony Pals. She had her pony. "Lightning," Pam called. "Come on, girl. We're going for a ride!"

But Lightning didn't come out of the shed. She didn't even turn around.

As Pam got closer she shouted, "Hey, Lightning, it's me. Pam. Didn't you hear me?"

Lightning still didn't turn around.

"We're going for a ride," Pam repeated.

Pam suddenly felt frightened. Even when her pony was munching on grass or hay, she always looked in the direction of Pam's voice.

Pam took a step into the shed. Lightning turned her head, put her ears back, and bared her teeth. It was the fiercest look Pam had ever seen on any pony's face. She was so startled by it that she let out a frightened yelp and ran out of the shed. Her heart pounded. What's wrong with my pony? she wondered. Is she angry at me?

I have to get help, Pam told herself.

First she ran to her father's animal clinic.

No one was there.

She ran to the house. As she burst into the kitchen she screamed. "Mom! Dad! Help! Something's wrong with Lightning."

Nobody answered her call. She ran upstairs. No one was there.

She decided to check her mother's office in the barn. As Pam was leaving the house through the kitchen she noticed a note on the table.

Pam, dear —
Dad and I took the twins to the Danbury Mall to get shoes. Back around five.
Love,
Mom

Pam's heart sank. There was no one to help her. She had to face this problem alone. If only Anna and Lulu hadn't ruined the Pony Pals, she thought. If only we didn't have a fight. . . .

She ran back to the run-in shed. Lightning still had her back to her. Pam spoke to Lightning in a calm, soothing voice. "Did I wake you up from a nightmare before?" she asked. "Well, everything's okay now. Let's go for a ride."

Lightning ignored her.

Pam stepped into the shed and the horrible thing happened again. Lightning turned on her with fierce eyes, bared teeth, and an angry snort.

Pam didn't scream this time. She knew that if she was going to figure out what was wrong with Lightning she had to remain calm.

The first question she asked herself was, "Is Lightning sick?"

Pam knew what Lightning looked like when she was sick and she didn't look like that now. Lightning's head wasn't drooping. Her coat didn't look feverish.

So if she isn't sick, Pam wondered, what's wrong? Then she remembered what Anna said, "Lightning must hate that you keep leaving her behind." And how Lulu said, "Lightning's smart. You can't fool her."

Pam also remembered the way Lightning stood watching at the fence the first time she rode Splash. What if Lightning knows that I'm taking Splash and Daisy out on the trail instead of her? Pam thought. She must be jealous. And now she's angry.

"I'm sorry I've been riding Splash and Daisy so much," Pam told Lightning. "And I'm sorry I didn't take you on the trail this weekend." Pam felt the tears streaming down her face. "Please forgive me."

Lightning whipped her tail around in a circle and snorted.

For the first time in her life Pam was afraid of her own pony.

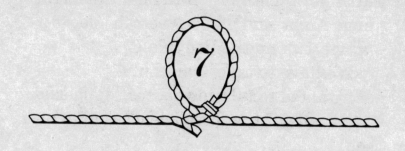

Crazy Pony

Pam sat on the grass near the shed and wiped the tears away with her shirtsleeve. She stared at Lightning. Her pony had gone crazy because she hadn't given her enough attention. Pam wished with all her heart that her friends were there to help her.

Then she heard Acorn's whinny and her friends' voices. At first she thought she was imagining them. But she saw that Anna and Lulu were really there, leading their ponies across the paddock.

Pam ran up to them. Before she could

catch her breath to tell them about Lightning, Anna said. "Pam, we can't let *anything* break up the Pony Pals."

"We have to talk," said Lulu.

"I wanted to talk to you, too," Pam said.

"I'm sorry!" the three friends said in unison.

Lulu and Anna were so happy that the fight was over that they laughed out loud. But their laughter stopped when they looked at Pam. "Something's wrong with Lightning," Pam said.

"What happened?" Anna asked.

"I was going to ride her," Pam began, "but Lightning, she . . . she's so mad at me. She won't leave the shed. It's like she's turned into a crazy pony! And it's all my fault."

"Start at the beginning and tell us everything," Lulu said.

While they led Acorn and Snow White to a side paddock, Pam told her friends everything that Lightning had done since she got home.

When Pam finished, Anna said, "Don't worry, Pam. We'll help you. We're Pony Pals. We have Pony Pal Power."

Then the three friends ran over to the shed. They observed Lightning and thought about what to do next.

"Here's an idea," said Lulu. "If Lightning is mad at you, maybe I should get her."

"Good thinking," Pam said. She handed the halter and lead rope to Lulu.

"Hi, Lightning," Lulu said as she walked toward her. "It's time to come out. Snow White's in the other paddock. She wants to play with you."

"Be careful, Lulu," Anna warned. "Go around so she can't kick you."

The moment Lulu stepped into the shed, Lightning turned on her with a fierce, angry look.

Lulu backed quickly away. "Sorry, Lightning," she said in a trembling voice.

"Lightning doesn't even look like Lightning," Anna said. "This is awful!"

"She won't let us near her," Lulu said.

"We'll have to get her to leave on her own," Anna said.

"But how?" Lulu asked.

"Food," said Pam. "Maybe she'll leave the shed for oats."

They all agreed that it was a good idea.

Pam ran to the barn. In a few minutes she was back with oats and carrots. She placed the bucket of oats at the edge of the shed. "Lightning, here's some good oats for you," she said in a cheery voice.

Lightning turned toward the sound of Pam's voice and sniffed the air for the sweet smell of oats.

"It's going to work," Anna whispered.

But at that instant, Lightning turned back toward the shed wall.

Pam moved the bucket of oats into the shed. Lightning kicked out at her with a back leg.

Pam ran to Anna and Lulu. "Lightning *never* kicks," she told them. "It's like she's turned into another pony. A mean one."

"Let's look at what we've figured out so far," Lulu suggested.

"Lightning won't let us in the shed," said Pam.

"And she won't come out," Lulu said.

"Maybe we should give her something to eat without going in," said Anna. "If we put a carrot on a stick we wouldn't have to go in the shed and she wouldn't have to leave."

"It's worth a try," Lulu agreed.

Pam broke a dead branch off the maple tree while Lulu unlaced one of her shoes. Anna used the shoelace to tie the carrot loosely to the end of the branch. Then Anna dangled the carrot out where Lightning could smell it. "Here's a treat for you, Lightning," she said.

Lightning turned her head toward Anna. But this time she didn't make the terrible face. Instead she quickly pulled the carrot off the branch. The girls let out sighs of relief.

"Well, now we're getting somewhere," said Lulu.

"Maybe you should try to go in now," Anna whispered to Pam, "while she's eating the carrot."

"But keep away from her legs," warned Lulu as she handed the halter and lead rope back to Pam.

Pam took a few steps into the shed before Lightning noticed her. But when she did, the pony dropped the carrot so she could snort angrily at Pam.

Pam rushed out of the shed. "Nothing we try is working," she told her friends.

"Don't give up, Pam," said Lulu. "We never give up."

"It's all my fault," said Pam.

"Maybe Lightning isn't mad at you," Anna said. "Maybe there's another reason she wants to stay in the shed."

"Maybe there's something in the shed that would keep her in there," added Lulu.

"Then we have to figure out what it is," Pam said

"Maybe there's a poisonous snake in the

straw," Anna said. "And Lightning is protecting us from getting bit."

"Then why hasn't *she* been bit?" asked Lulu.

"Maybe she *has* been bit," Pam said with alarm. "And that's why she's acting so weird."

"She doesn't have a swollen leg or anything," said Lulu. "And she's standing so still. I think she'd be jumping all over the place if she got bit."

Just then Fat Cat came walking by the girls. She was headed toward the shed.

"Catch her," Anna yelled. "Lightning's acting so crazy she might step on her."

But Fat Cat was already under the legs of the angry pony.

"Come back, Fat Cat!" Pam yelled.

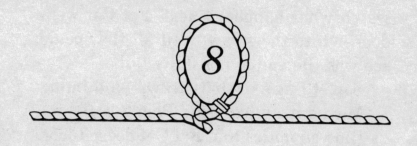

The Baby-sitter

Anna wanted to run into the shed to save the cat from the dangerous pony. But Lulu grabbed Anna's arm and held her back.

Meanwhile, the pony stayed perfectly still and calm. Lightning didn't snort at the cat. She didn't make an angry face. She didn't kick.

"Maybe it's just people she won't let go in the shed," said Lulu.

Pam crouched down. "Look," she said, "Fat Cat's digging at the straw."

Anna and Lulu squatted beside Pam to watch what happened next. Fat Cat went deeper into the straw until all they could see was the end of her fluffy tail.

"Something's in that straw," said Lulu.

"Maybe it's mice," said Pam.

"Did you notice that Fat Cat doesn't look so fat anymore?" asked Anna.

"Kittens!" the Pony Pals said in unison.

"That must be it," said Anna. "Fat Cat's had her babies in there."

They waited quietly to see what would happen next.

"Oh-hh, look," Pam whispered.

Fat Cat walked out of the shed between Lightning's legs. She held a tiny kitten in her mouth.

"It's true!" Pam cried. "Lightning was protecting Fat Cat's kittens!"

"And she didn't want us to step on them by mistake," said Lulu.

"Let's follow Fat Cat and see where she puts the kittens," said Anna.

"I hope she doesn't hide them," Lulu said. "Some mother cats like to be private."

"Let's set up a box and food for her in the feed room closet," said Pam. "It's private in there."

"I hope it works," said Lulu.

Anna and Pam ran toward the barn. Lulu followed Fat Cat.

Pam laid an old blanket in an empty cardboard box and put it in the closet. Anna put a bowl of cat food and fresh water near the door to the feed room Then they went into an empty stall to watch.

A few seconds later Fat Cat walked into the barn, still carrying the tiny kitten. Lulu was spying on her from a safe distance. Fat Cat walked right by the feed room. Pam and Anna mouthed "Oh, no" to one another.

Suddenly, Fat Cat turned around and marched right back to the feed room.

Lulu went into the stall with Pam and Anna. In a few seconds they saw Fat Cat

leave the feed room. There wasn't a kitten in her mouth.

The Pony Pals hit silent high fives. Then they tiptoed into the feed room to take a peek at the newborn kitten.

"It looks like a baby mouse," Anna whispered. "It's so tiny."

"I wonder how many more there'll be," said Lulu.

"Let's go back and watch," suggested Pam.

The Pony Pals sat in the grass by the shed and watched as, one by one, Fat Cat pulled her kittens out of the straw and carried them to the barn. Between kitten number 2 and kitten number 3 Lightning turned her head to the Pony Pals. Her ears were relaxed, her teeth didn't show, and her eyes were calm.

"She trusts us now," said Lulu.

"And she's not mad at me," added Pam.

When Fat Cat scampered away from the

shed with kitten number 5 in her mouth, Lightning lowered her head and sniffed at the straw. Satisfied that all the kittens were gone, she turned around and walked out of the shed.

"Look how stiff she is," said Lulu.

"It's hard to stay still that long," Anna said.

Pam ran over to Lightning and gave her a big hug. "I'm so proud of you," she said. "You're the most wonderful pony in the world." Lightning nuzzled her shoulder like always.

Then Pam's pony galloped around the paddock. She shook her mane and whinnied as if to say, "I did a good job. Now I want to have some fun."

Snow White and Acorn ran to the fence that separated their paddock from Lightning's and whinnied at her.

Pam opened the gate that separated the two paddocks. Acorn and Snow White ran through to join Lightning in the field.

The girls laughed. "They're like us," said Lulu. "They love to have fun together."

A few minutes later Pam's parents drove up the driveway. The three girls raced to the car. They couldn't wait to tell the Crandals about Lightning's baby-sitting job.

But there was no way to tell anyone anything until the twins showed off their new shoes and the two toy horses they'd gotten for their horse collection.

Jill held out hers. "It's an Arabian," she said. "Just like the black stallion."

"Mine's a Shetland," bragged Jack. "Like Acorn."

The girls told the story of what had happened with Fat Cat and Lightning. The twins wanted to go see the kittens right away. But their parents and the Pony Pals said they should wait a couple of hours.

"If we go in too soon," Lulu told the twins, "Fat Cat might move them someplace where we won't be able to see them at all."

The twins went to their room to add the toy ponies to their collection.

"So how did Daisy do at group trail riding?" Mrs. Crandal asked Pam.

"Not too good," Pam answered. "She needs a lot of work, Mom. That pony is too easily distracted on the trail. And she's so slow. It's the opposite problem of Splash."

"I hope my new ponies aren't going to be problem ponies," Mrs. Crandal said. She sighed. "They've been a lot more work than I thought they'd be. I'm really depending on you, Pam."

"I know, Mom," Pam said.

"Did you write up about the trail ride on Daisy's training chart?" she asked.

"Not yet," Pam said.

Anna and Lulu went to the barn with Pam. Pam made the new entry on Daisy's chart.

on the trail in group	nw
comments	doesn't keep up with other ponies; easily distracted

Anna and Lulu looked at the ponies' training charts.

"I didn't know how much responsibility you had," said Lulu.

"Working two ponies every day takes a lot of time," said Anna. "You're lucky schoolwork's easy for you."

"I told my mom I wanted the job," Pam said. "And I do. But I want to be with you, too. I've got a problem."

"*You* don't have a problem," Lulu said.

"I don't?!" Pam exclaimed.

"We all have a problem," said Anna. "This is a Pony Pal Problem. So we'll all have to solve it."

Pam wasn't so sure they could solve her problem. But it was nice to know her friends were on her side.

Broken Brownies

The Pony Pals met at their school lockers the next morning.

"I've been thinking about my problem — I mean *our* problem," Pam said. "How would you two like a part-time weekend job?"

Anna and Lulu smiled at one another.

"Would this job involve schooling ponies?" Lulu asked.

"Two ponies that happen to belong to the Crandal Riding School," added Anna with a giggle.

Pam laughed. "Exactly," she said.

"It's a great idea," Lulu agreed. "If three of us work, it won't take so long."

"And we'll still have time to trail ride with our ponies," said Anna.

"Will you do it?" Pam asked. "It'd only be one hour on Saturday. And one on Sunday. And my mom said she'd pay you, too." Pam hoped with all her heart that her friends would say yes.

"It'll be good experience," said Lulu.

"It makes sense," said Anna. "If we work together we have time to ride together."

"And I could really use some help," said Pam.

"But I don't know how to train a pony," said Lulu. "Especially one that's strong-willed like Splash."

"Together we can do it," said Pam. "This Saturday we'll work on Splash and trail riding. I think we should have a lesson plan."

"Remember what Splash did last time!"

groaned Anna. "That was awful."

"This calls for three ideas," said Lulu.

"Maybe we could meet right after school," suggested Pam. "But it has to be a short meeting because I've got to get to work."

"I'm raking the yard for my grandmother after school," said Lulu. "But I could go to a meeting first." She smiled at Pam. "My grandmother pays me for yard work. I'm saving for a new saddle, too."

"Is today one of your tutor days?" Pam asked Anna. Pam knew that Anna was dyslexic and that she had a tutor twice a week to help her with reading.

"Yes," Anna answered, "but not until four o'clock."

The Pony Pals agreed to go to the Off-Main Diner for a meeting right after school.

When the Pony Pals left school that afternoon they rushed down Main Street, turned on Belgo Road, and ran over to the Off-Main Diner. Pam pulled open the big glass door. "Your mom's here," she told Anna.

Lulu sniffed the air as she walked in. "And she just made brownies."

Anna's mother owned the Off-Main Diner and was famous for her chewy chocolate brownies. The three girls took deep breaths of the warm, sweet smell of cooling brownies. They followed the smell to the counter.

Mrs. Harley looked up from cutting a huge pan of brownies. "I'm so glad you girls stopped by," she said. "I've just cut these brownies. There are some broken ones that I didn't quite know what to do with."

"We'll try to help you out, Mom," teased Anna.

The girls carried a plate of broken brownies and glasses of milk to their favorite booth in the back of the diner.

Pam opened the meeting by saying, "Our problem is how to train Splash to trail ride in a group. Lulu, go first."

"Okay," Lulu said. "Listen to this."

Don't take our ponies on the trail with Splash. For the first lesson bring just one other pony. A quiet one like Daisy.

"That's a great idea," said Pam.

"And it leads right into my idea," said Anna.

She laid a drawing on the table.

"I agree that our own ponies should all stay behind when we train the ponies," Anna said. "But Acorn, Snow White, and Lightning should all be together. That way they'll have one another and none of them will get upset when we leave."

Pam and Lulu agreed with Anna.

"My idea is about *how* to work with Splash," Pam said.

She read:

I ride Splash. Lulu walks next to Splash and directs him with a lead rope.

"That's a terrific idea," Lulu told Pam.

"I checked with my mother about it," Pam said. "She thought it was a good idea, too."

"Does your mother mind if we all work at your job on weekends?" asked Anna.

"She wonders why she didn't think of it herself," said Pam. "I just hope our plan works. Her new riding students start in two weeks."

Back on the Trail

Monday, after school, Pam worked in the ring with Splash and Daisy. Lightning watched the lesson from her paddock.

When Pam finished with the new ponies, her mother said, "I'll get the tack off these two. You go spend some time with Lightning."

Pam didn't need a lead rope to bring in her pony. The instant Lightning saw Pam coming in her direction she raced to the fence.

Every day that week, Pam worked the

new ponies. Then she took Lightning for a trail ride.

Saturday morning, Pam met Anna and Lulu as they rode off Pony Pal Trail.

"What do we do first?" Anna asked Pam.

"Go see the new kittens!" Pam answered. "Wait until you see. They're getting so cute."

After they let Acorn and Snow White out in the paddock with Lightning, the three girls ran to the barn.

They went right to the feed room and looked in the closet. Fat Cat was nursing her kittens in the cardboard box. The mother cat looked up at the three girls and purred.

"She's so proud," Anna whispered.

"Are all her babies going to be gray?" asked Lulu.

"There's one under her leg that looks like it'll be mostly white," Pam said.

"Is Fat Cat still doing mice patrol?" Anna asked.

"You bet," Pam chuckled. "She's a hard working mother *and* a mouse chaser."

"Pretty soon she'll have five helpers," said Lulu.

"We're going to give three of the kittens away," said Pam.

"So she'll have *two* helpers," Anna giggled. "Just like Pam and her *two* helpers."

"Okay, helpers," Pam said to Anna and Lulu. "Let's get to work."

With three girls saddling two ponies, Splash and Daisy were ready in a few minutes. Next, the girls led the ponies to the beginning of Pony Pal Trail.

Acorn and Snow White noticed the parade of girls and ponies. But they turned right back to grazing.

"I told you our ponies would be fine as long as they were together," Anna commented.

"Splash and I will lead," Pam said when they reached the beginning of Pony Pal Trail.

"And I'll walk next to you," Lulu said.

"Anna, make Daisy keep up with us," Pam said. "Don't let her be a slowpoke."

Splash wanted to trot or canter right away. But Pam and Lulu insisted that he keep to the walk. Splash calmed down.

"Good work, Splash," Pam said.

When it was time to move him up into the trot, Pam told Lulu, "Go back and work with Daisy. Get her to keep up with Splash."

Pam gave the direction and Splash moved right into a spirited trot. After letting him continue for awhile, Pam halted the pony. She was happy with how quickly he was responding to her. She wondered if Daisy had kept up. Pam turned in her saddle to see that the golden pony was exactly a pony length behind her. Perfect spacing for the trail!

"So far we're doing great," Pam called back to Anna and Lulu. "Now let's put Daisy first."

They turned the ponies around so Daisy would be in the lead.

"This is the hardest part of today's lesson for Splash," said Pam. "He's going to want to rush ahead."

"I'll help," Lulu said as she walked over to Splash.

Anna started Daisy off at the walk.

But Splash wanted to move right into a faster gait. When he started to trot, Pam and Lulu moved him around in a little circle. Every time Splash wanted to rush ahead, the girls moved him in another small circle.

"He'll get sick of these circles," Pam said. "Then he'll behave."

After the fifth circle, Splash finally calmed down and kept to the pace Daisy set.

"There's your mom," Lulu called back to Pam. Pam looked beyond Daisy and saw her mother walking toward them.

The three girls and two ponies stopped in front of Mrs. Crandal.

"I came out to see how it's going," she said.

Anna leaned over and patted Daisy's neck. "Daisy's doing terrific," she said.

"And Splash is staying in line a lot better," Pam reported.

"Show me," Mrs. Crandal said, "without Lulu's help. Go down to our end of the trail and back." She pointed to a big rock next to the trail. "Lulu and I will watch you from up there."

Pam was worried that Splash wouldn't do as well with people watching. But once the demonstration began she thought only about riding Splash. He worked with her better than ever.

When they completed the run, Pam brought Splash to a halt in front of the rock. "That was very good," Mrs. Crandal said. "You girls worked those ponies beautifully. You can bring them in now."

On the way home, Lulu rode Splash and Pam walked alongside the pony. After they let the new ponies out in the paddock, the Pony Pals brought their own ponies to the barn. It was time to saddle up and go for a Pony Pal trail ride.

"Now we can ride over to Mudge Road and play in that old house on the Ridley farm," Pam said.

While they tacked up their ponies, the girls talked about the house and what they'd do there. They were ready to head out on their ride when Mrs. Crandal came into the barn. Pam noticed that she was carrying three envelopes.

Mrs. Crandal handed an envelope to Anna and another to Lulu. "For your work today, girls," she said. "You did a fine job."

"Thank you," Lulu said.

"It was neat," said Anna.

"I hope I can call on you again sometime," she said.

"I thought we were working tomorrow, too," Anna said.

"That won't be necessary," Mrs. Crandal

said. She handed Pam an envelope. "This is your week's pay, dear," she said.

"Thanks, Mom," Pam said. She folded the envelope and tucked it in her back jeans pocket.

"You were a good worker, Pam," her mother told her. "It was very hard for awhile, but you stuck it out. It's a job well done and I'm proud of you."

"Is my job over?" Pam asked.

"Yes," Mrs. Crandal said. "My new students start next week, so they'll be working the ponies. I might need you to give Splash and Daisy a refresher course once in a while. But for now they'll be very satisfactory school ponies. Thanks to you."

When Pam's mother left, Pam turned to Lulu and Anna. "I'm out of a job," she said. "Do you know what that means?"

"It means you won't have to work after school," Lulu said.

"Or on weekends," added Anna.

The Pony Pals raised their hands to hit

high fives, but Anna dropped her hand before they did it. "Not having a job also means you won't be able to buy a new saddle," she said.

Pam thought about that for a second. Then she said, "I'll have enough money for it someday. Right now I'd rather be a Pony Pal with my old saddle."

The Pony Pals hit their high fives and shouted, "*All right!*" Lightning whinnied and nuzzled into Pam's shoulder.

Pam lay her head on Lightning's neck. "Today we're going for a nice long ride," she told her pony. "You, me, and our Pony Pals."

Dear Reader,

I am having a lot of fun researching and writing books about the Pony Pals. I've met many interesting kids and adults who love ponies. And I've visited some wonderful ponies at homes, farms, and riding schools.

Before writing Pony Pals I wrote fourteen novels for children and young adults. Four of these were honored by Children's Choice Awards.

I live in Sharon, Connecticut, with my husband, Lee, and our dog, Willie. Our daughter is all grown up and has her own apartment in New York City.

Besides writing novels I like to draw, paint, garden and swim. I didn't have a pony when I was growing up, but I have always loved them and dreamt about riding. Now I take riding lessons on a horse named Saz. To learn more, visit my Web site: www.jeannebetancourt.com.

I like reading and writing about ponies as much as I do riding. Which proves to me that you don't have to ride a pony to love them. And you certainly don't need a pony to be a Pony Pal.

Happy Reading,

Jeanne Betancourt

Pony Pals

Be a Pony Pal!®

Available wherever you buy books, or use this order form.

....